Little Red Hen

Retold by Lyn Calder

Illustrated by Jeffrey Severn

For Jean, Tamara, and Bill Jr. —J.S.

A GOLDEN BOOK • NEW YORK

Western Publishing Company, Inc., Racine, Wisconsin 53404

One day Little Red Hen was scratching around
in her garden when she found some grains of wheat.

"Who will help me plant this wheat?" asked
Little Red Hen.

"Not I," said Duck.

"Not I," said Cat.

"Not I," said Dog.

"Then I will plant the wheat myself,"
said Little Red Hen.
     And she did.

Day by day the wheat grew. When it was tall and yellow, Little Red Hen asked, "Who will help me cut the wheat?"

"Not I," said Duck.
"Not I," said Cat.
"Not I," said Dog.

"Then I will cut the wheat myself,"
said Little Red Hen.
  And she did.

Once Little Red Hen had cut the wheat, she asked, "Who will help me thresh the wheat?"

"Not I," said Duck.

"Not I," said Cat.

"Not I," said Dog.

"Then I will thresh the wheat myself,"
said Little Red Hen.
And she did.

The wheat had to be ground into flour.
"Who will help me take the wheat to the miller for grinding?" asked Little Red Hen.

"Not I," said Duck.

"Not I," said Cat.

"Not I," said Dog.

"Then I will take the wheat to the miller myself," said Little Red Hen.

And she did.

When Little Red Hen returned with the flour,
she asked, "Who will help me make the dough
and bake the bread?"

"Not I," said Duck.

"Not I," said Cat.

"Not I," said Dog.

"Then I will make the dough and bake
the bread myself," said Little Red Hen.
And she did.

Finally the bread was ready. "Who will help me eat this warm and tasty bread?" asked Little Red Hen.

"I *will!*" said Duck.

"I *will!*" said Cat.

"I *will!*" said Dog.

"Oh, no!" said Little Red Hen. "I will eat
the bread myself."
And she did.